ALONG CAME A SPIDER: Prequel Novella One of The Legends Chronicles
Copyright © 2017 by K.M. Robinson.

Published by Crescent Sea Publishing.
www.crescentseapublishing.com

Cover designed by Reading Transforms.
Image copyright © K.M. Robinson Photography.
Interior graphics by Reading Transforms.

K.M. ROBINSON

ALONG CAME A SPIDER

The Legends Chronicles

LITTLE MISS MUFFET

Little Miss Muffet sat on her tuffet,
eating her curds and whey.
Along came a spider
who sat down beside her
and frightened Miss Muffet away.

CHAPTER 1

"FIND HER...IF YOU CAN." THE WORDS SCROLLED across the screen of the device before crackling away.

Fet looked down in disgust, tempted to throw the device across the room. Instead, she tucked it into the pocket of her skirt and stood so quickly she nearly toppled the screen in front of her.

The light from the screen bounced off the ceiling of the dark room, lit only by glowing computers. The display wall illuminated the right side of Fet's coworker harshly as she looked up from where she was secretly slipping into the innermost workings of a government technology system for her superiors.

"Fet?" the girl asked her boss.

"Never mind, T," she said as softly as the hard edge that resided in her voice would allow. "Go back to work, I'll handle this."

"What's wrong?" a tall, lanky guy in glasses asked from across the room.

"It doesn't matter, BB, I'm handling it." Fet glared,

flicking her wrist in his direction. She had no time for his emotional attachment to her unexpected problem. Her eyes darted to where the message had been on her screen only moments before.

"You tell us right now, or..."

"Or *what?*" Fet bellowed "What will you do, *BB*? Hack me?"

"Ha. I'd like to see him try," T snickered.

"Shut up, T. Clearly something is happening here and she's not telling us. If I have to take this to Peep, I will," the boy threatened to run to his girlfriend.

Fet raised her eyebrow in a challenge. She knew what BB did not: their leader wasn't there.

"Where *is* Peep, anyway? I haven't seen her all day," T asked, looking around the room as the others stirred from their stations.

Fet's device buzzed in her pocket, lighting up against her thigh. All eyes dragged across the room to focus on the slight vibrating sound that they were all entirely tuned-in to. Sliding her fingers along her hip, she retrieved the technology. Propping her elbow against her body, she leaned to the side to read the new message. A video queued up and BB was at her side before she could keep the audio from filling the room.

"Muffet," the voice filled the room. "Don't do it!"

The girl's voice was cut off as a slap sent her flying to the floor. BB gasped, his eyes widening as he realized what he was seeing. T grabbed at Fet's arm, jerking her away from the device. She regained her balance in time for an off-camera voice to pick up the message.

"Hello again, Muffet. I see you received my first message. So glad we could connect." The digital voice sang in a monotone registry pitched far too high to be within the acceptable range of human hearing. "If you want your lackey alive, crack the code, fix the problem. I'll be in touch with your first puzzle."

"Muffet, don't. Get out! *Now!*"

Another crack sounded just before the screen fizzled out.

"Run a trace," Fet commanded, sending BB and the others scattering across the room to their computers. "They have Peep and we have to find her."

"But, Fet, if they have Peep, why are they contacting us?" T asked, fingers flying over her keyboard as she tried to glance up as she worked, her brown hair falling in her face. She tucked a random braid behind her ear, its tie matching her deep red lipstick.

"Because they don't know *Peep is in charge*. Peep hides behind *me*, you know that, T." Fet criticized, "I'm the face of the Legends...or the *handle*, I guess. They're using *her* to get to *me*. They don't realize they already have the girl they want."

"And let's keep it that way," BB cautioned angrily. Concern for his girlfriend's wellbeing pulled tightly on the corners of his eyes and pounded out through his fingers as they flew across the keyboard.

"Walk away. Now." Words suddenly scrawled across the screen still in Fet's hand.

Glancing around the room, Fet casually walked over to T and grabbed her by the collar.

"Keep them occupied. I'll be in touch," Fet hissed, throwing the other girl back into her seat. The small girl was too shocked to fight back, simply nodding in acknowledgement.

Fet wound her way through the room toward the door, the others not bothering to look up as their search through the deepest crevices of the dark web occupied their thoughts. She slipped the door open silently and crept into the outside room. A blue glow filled the space, feeling much more open than the confines of the inner office of the hidden building. Sounds of clicking filled the air as the new recruits continued their assigned tasks, sitting in their final destinations before being accepted into the Legends. The next step for them was through the door Fet had just vacated.

Several heads looked up as she passed, her pink plaid skirt swishing as she stomped through the room, but they didn't say a word as she thundered through. Unlooping the necklace that hung over her chest, she plugged it into the device sending her messages. The other end coiled behind her and around to the opposite hip where she kept her secondary device. Typing code into her alternate tech, she kicked the door shut behind her, slamming it against the wall. She never *had* minded scaring the recruits.

"What have you gotten yourself into, Bo Peep?" she muttered as she snaked her way down the streets and alleyways until she reached a spot where she could escape detection. Turning off all of the cameras from her device, she ensured she would be undetectable.

"Now what?" she mumbled to herself.

"What exactly are you doing?"

Fet's fist flew up in an effort to defend herself against the man who was about to attack her. There was no way she'd let herself be taken like Peep had been.

"Whoa, *easy there*, killer." The man stepped backwards, hands raised in front of him. Fet was uncertain if it was in surrender or in defense.

"What do you want?" Fet stage whispered through bared teeth to convey her annoyance while still keeping from being overheard from the streets.

"You lit out of there like your pigtails were on fire," the man said, appraising her.

Fet looked him over for the first time. This leather jacket accentuated his long dark hair, short on one side, long on the other. His combat boots were taller than hers, laced nearly to his knees. All he was missing was a couple of facial piercings and he could have passed as a modern day music star.

"I don't know you." Fet said, standing. Turning away, she waved him off and tried to leave.

"I'm a trainee...from the recruitment class. You've worked with me before." He followed after her.

"Don't care." She continued her escape.

"You *should*," he snapped at her, reaching out for her arm. "I'm the best help you've got."

"I don't need help." She slapped his hand away, holding back the punch she wanted to land on his face.

"Yes, you do."

"I don't *want* your help," she corrected.

"I was right by the door, I heard it all. This is big. Peep is missing and you're *supposed* to be on your own finding her. But no one knows about *me*," he shrugged, "So let me help. I'll be your secret weapon."

"Can you even hack, *little one*?" she said spitefully, hoping to insult him. He stood a head above her at least, but couldn't possibly have half her talent.

"Better than you," he sneered, finally a spark in his gaze.

"Dream on," she chastised, pushing him away from her.

A moment later her device buzzed against her thigh. Pulling it from its pocket, she discovered a message.

"Told you," it read.

When she slowly turned, the dark clothed man was waving his device to her.

"Can we try this again, *Muffet?*"

"You know...?" she asked, her face going slack.

"Of *course* I know who you are, Muffet," he said, informing her that he knew her as more than just Fet. "I've been following you for a long time. You're the entire reason I signed up for the Legends."

Fet stepped closer as she realized this was no ordinary recruit.

"Who are you?"

"Spider," he answered, as if his name alone should send her running to hide in a corner.

Instead, her fist slammed into his shoulder, just missing his neck.

"You destroyed the Wall job last year!" she screamed, her anger overtaking her sense of self-preservation. "You cost me a year's wages!"

"Oh, get over yourself, Muffet. To the victor go the spoils." He smirked at her.

Gritting her teeth, she backed up to launch another attack.

"Knock it off, Muffet. We can fight later. Right now, we have to find Peep." He grabbed her airborne wrist, holding off her punch. Twisting, she pulled away.

The chances of finding someone as skilled as Spider,

much less one that no one knew was involved, were non-existent.

"Fine," she acquiesced.

"Good, I already pulled the data from your device." He smiled, tipping his technology back and forth once again. "Your first task came in during your assault, by the way."

Her eyes narrowed at the boy, but she allowed her fingers to travel the familiar path to the device, retrieving it and swiping it to life.

You will perform a series of tasks. Go to the Hub. On the roof, you will find an access panel to the network. Crack the code.

"What does it say?" Spider asked innocently. With his chin tipped slightly away from her, he looked out under his veil of dark hair on one side, eyes wide.

"Aren't bugs supposed to have big eyes? *Look for yourself.*" Fet waved her hand to dismiss him.

"You're in charge here, Fet. This is your mission and I have to keep a low profile. I'll follow your lead," Spider said, falling into step behind her as she turned and marched toward the local center of technology.

"If you actually meant that, you'd leave so I wouldn't have to squash you," she said angrily, her boot crunching against the gravel louder than usual.

"Don't be so petty, Muffet," he growled. "You need me."

As if to make his point, he leaned into her, brushing

his leather jacket against her arm. Sighing loudly, she elbowed him, driving him just far enough away to create a slight separation between them. Ordinarily she might be worried her device was being cloned, but since he had *already* done that, the proximity only served to anger her.

CHAPTER 2

"GO HIDE, PEST," SHE ADDRESSED HIM as the building fell into view. Spider slipped behind a hedge of bushes, blending into the dark branches as Fet made her way to the metallic grey structure.

Launching herself onto the stairs, she swung up onto the ledge. Kicking her feet off of the stairway railing, Fet steadied herself on the edge of the building, disappearing from Spider's limited view.

"There," she muttered as she located the panel once safely on the roof. Pulling open the covering, she searched the screen looking for the coded message. Finding nothing, she rocked back on her heels.

After a moment, Fet grabbed a rock. She dragged its edge along the screen. Peeling the blank piece back, she revealed a secondary screen, blinking alive with its newfound freedom.

As she began to type, a code appeared on the screen, racing as she decoded its message. Fet's brow creased, her frown deepening as she deciphered the symbols. The code was tough—not even many of the Legends could crack it given the opportunity.

"This doesn't make sense," she announced to herself as her fingers flew over the board. "What is this?"

"Finish it." The command scrolled across the screen, interrupting the coding.

"But this will..." She didn't finish her thought, knowing it would fall on deaf ears, if she could be heard *at all.*

Her fingers hesitated, hovering just over the keys. With final keystroke, it would be done and the entire town would be plunged into darkness as the power cut off: real life consequences for online puzzles.

Knowing it would cause pure chaos in the town built to survive off of technology, she hit the last button, breaking the code. The screen shattered into a million digital pieces as a new screen reassembled in its wake.

Fet heard the collective gasp from the building, the windows having all been open to let in the spring air. She knew their devices had all gone offline, leaving them defenseless. An administrator screamed directions, furious at their employees, somewhere below her. Miraculously, the screen in front of her and her own device still remained active.

A new cipher glowed within the screen, announcing its need for a new manipulation of code. Fet could feel the heat rising through her collar, creeping up into her neck. If Fet was one of those girls whose body knew how to sweat, it would have been doing it. Instead, the flush snaked up her back and burst through the back of her skull, making her incredibly aware that this plan went further than simply getting her–*Muffet*, ultimate hacker, and perceived Legends leader–to the enemy. She would not be able to save Peep without the entire world knowing something was happening.

After her first string of attempts failed, she pulled out her own device. Leaning over the edge of the wall, she glanced down, looking for Spider. Did she want to see his reaction? Was she making sure he was safe? She didn't know why she would concern herself with such an annoyance as the hacker that ruined her big job not too long ago. When she couldn't find him, she turned back to her task. She'd worry about his abandonment later.

On her device was the code needed to complete the sequence and activate the next prompt. Keying it into the screen, she waited for her next directive. It flashed across the screen as she shoved her accessory into her pocket and leaped over the edge of the building, gripping the ledge.

Her feet found their mark and she lowered herself onto the steps. Racing back down the side of the building, she timed her escape so the watchmen wouldn't see her. People raced around outside, the watchmen looking busy, though clearly they had no training to fix the problem. A group of men and women burst through the doors, attempting to right the situation. Fet knew the chaos inside would be worse as the employees worked to turn the power system back on. Without the use of their devices, they were practically helpless.

The Coats, the elite few in charge of the technology, would be sent for and deployed to the site to oversee the attempts to turn the power structure back on. Fet needed to be long gone when they arrived. If she was detected, she would be arrested on the spot and detained indefinitely.

She tripped as she crashed through the bushes. Gravity pulled her forward and she threw her hands up to protect her face. Instead of finding gravel, her hands wrapped tightly within the slick confines of Spider's open jacket as he caught her, her hands brushing along his chest. Swinging her around, he countered the force of her fall as she gripped onto his coat tightly. Hanging upside down, she could feel Spider's arms wrap around her protectively. For a moment she hung, suspended in air with him until he continued the loop, arcing her back up to her feet. Tugging on her arm, he shouted quietly as they ran, "What did you do?"

The demand in his voice switched on her defensive tone as she wriggled out of his grasp and ran beside him. "The code turned off the power system, everything is down."

"No kidding, Fet. My device went down too."

"Mine still works, but I imagine that was the plan," Fet said, surprised as Spider matched her sharp turn without missing a step. Together they raced away from the Hub.

"Now what?" he asked.

"Now we have to find a Irex operating system," Fet answered, trying not to gasp as they ran.

"They haven't made an Irex in..."

"I know," Fet interrupted bruskly. "It would be in a museum if we had any of those left."

Over the years, it seemed the entire world had gone through digitalization, including three-dimensional renderings of ancient, and more recently-ancient, artifacts. To find an actual machine with an Irex operating system would be a miracle.

"There was one in the Hub," Spider offered, thinking out loud.

"Thanks, that's helpful," Fet chastised him. As she turned her head to glare, one of her pigtails whipped against her face, making her eyes sting.

"Down," Spider hissed, disrupting her train of thought as they both crashed to the ground. On hands and knees, Spider reached his arm around Fet, covering her shoulders as if the move alone could keep her from being seen. Their bodies shook with silent, heavy breaths as the watchmen rushed passed.

"We need to go another way," Fet whispered harshly.

"But where?" Spider answered, still too close for comfort. "Where are we going?"

"I know a place where there might be an Irex, but you're not going to like it. Come on." Fet stood to her feet the moment the watchmen had passed. Her short skirt swished around her as she turned, catching Spider's eye. He followed along behind her, forcing himself to keep pace as she dashed away.

"YOU HAVE TO BE KIDDING." SPIDER SAID, looking up the face of the cliff.

"Aren't spiders supposed to be good at climbing?" Fet taunted, extending her arm to grab the first stone.

"It's so steep it's practically inverted." Spider's eyes were wide as Fet lifted herself off the ground.

"That's why it's perfect," Fet called over her shoulder as she scaled the rock wall. "No one ever bothers it."

"The fact that it's in the middle of nowhere might have something to do with it," Spider called to her as he forced himself to latch onto the first handhold.

Fet was out of sight a moment later, scrambling over the side to the hidden entrance. The cave was dark, lit only by the blue screens housed inside. It had its own power system, far removed from the eyes of the government. The rock facade gave way to old-time luxury; metallic walls with a ventilation system circulating air to keep the machinery at the right temperature. A lighting system was mounted to the ceiling, but Fet didn't bother turning it on.

"Back here," she called when she heard Spider enter. She glanced up just in time to see his face fall in shock.

"Once they started the Upgrade, our grandparents started collecting the older machines. Not everything was saved, but there is a massive amount of technology here from over the years."

"This is a Hydren." Spider announced gleefully, the shock and reverence clear in his voice as he eyed a machine once he had recovered for the surprise of finding what he had been told the government had destroyed long ago.

"You want some time alone with the computer or are you actually going to help?" Fet glanced at him. He brushed his hair back behind his ear and tore himself away from the system. Moving further back, he wandered through the technology. He was going in the wrong direction, but Fet didn't bother to correct him.

After a few minutes of wandering, she located the

console she was looking for. She started it up. The machine silently flickered to life, adding a bright glow to the back corner of the room.

"You found it," Spider's quiet voice in her ear caused Fet to jump, nearly colliding with her conspirator's face.

"Watch it!" he yelped as he jumped back. His back ran into another console, nearly toppling it. At the last second he whirled, catching it with cat-like reflexes. Perhaps he had been hasty in choosing his handle.

Fet started relaying the previous code into the machine, adding her own code so the machine could understand the first. Removing her necklace again, she connected her device to the old operating system to help speed the process.

At the slight buzzing sound, they both looked to the device Fet had set on the table next to the console.

"Hand over control of the Irex to me," it read.

"They want the Irex?" Fet breathed. The Irex system has a series of flaws that forced the discontinuation of the production of the system long ago, but it had one attribute; it was unhackable and could control almost any system outside of itself. The government had initially used the Irex to oversee the lesser operating systems, but had worried what would happen if it had been in the wrong hands and the government could not regain control. All subsequent systems had been built with backdoors to avoid such problems.

"You're not really going to give them the Irex, are you?"

"What choice do we have? We have to get Peep back."

"I know she's your friend, Fet, but you're not going to give control over to these people for someone as unimportant as Peep, are you?"

Spider didn't need to know just how important Peep actually was. Afraid he would try to stop her, she knew he *did* need to know why she was giving it over.

"I have the backdoor," she announced as she began the code sequence to ready the transfer of power.

"What?" Spider looked genuinely shocked.

"Well, I know where to find it anyway," she added. "It will take a little time, but we can shut it down."

"There are no back doors, Fet. What are you talking about?"

"It helps to have had contact with the creator," Fet said nonchalantly, typing the last of the code. Picking up her device, she responded to the message, waiting for the transfer information.

Spider looked like his mind was being torn into a million pieces, each one following a trail of possibilities. Finally he shook his head, clearing away the shock. "First the ancient machines, now a backdoor. You surprised me, Fet....*for once.*"

Fet's arm swung around behind her in an attempt to hit him. She hadn't missed the condescending sarcasm in his voice. He may have had her in his sights all this time, but he was still not *better* than her.

"Transfer complete," the screen read before going blank.

A new screen popped up in its place and Fet watched as Peep's captor took over manipulating the machine. There was no way to prevent her from watching their every move now as code streamed across the interface.

Suddenly everything froze and Fet rose out of her chair. There it was: the next command.

CHAPTER 3

"THE WHITE COATS ARE AT THE HUB. BREAK INTO The Lab while they are gone and destroy it if you want your friend back." The screen read.

"Destroy it?" Fet asked in horror.

"How do they expect us to do that?" Spider hissed behind her, raking his hands through his hair, only the tips of his pale fingers visible around his black leather fingerless gloves as Fet turned to face him.

"Do they expect us to blow it up?" he asked.

"I don't know, but we have to go," Fet answered, twirling her own blonde pigtail in her hands. Standing, she threw one last look at the Irex, coding scrolling across the screen.

The sun was blinding as they exited the cave. Fet scrambled down the face of the cliff. She had only made the trip several times during her life, but she would never reveal to Spider that the climb terrified her. Spider's foot slipped, forcing gravity to help him the rest of the way to the ground. Fet reached out her hand and steadied him as his feet collided with the earth, miraculously leaving him upright.

"Let's go," she announced as she took off, leaving Spider in her wake. Suddenly she felt a sharp electrical burst against her hip.

"Stop," the screen read.

Eyes darting up, she focused ahead of her, confused, searching for an answer.

"*You*," she growled, turning on her heels, when she realized what had happened.

"I'm helping you, best not to leave me behind." Spider sneered, slipping his device back into his own pocket.

"If you *ever...*" Fet started her tirade, but he stopped her with a raised hand.

"We don't have time for your lectures, Muffet. Save the dramatic flair for your work." He walked passed her at an accelerated clip, his jab about her coding flourishes stinging more than it should. Fet had always taken great pride in her work, and somehow he found a way to diminish it.

Running beyond him, she set the pace for their journey to The Lab. They were both struggling for breath when they arrived, the sun lower in the sky, but still bright. The large building had several guards posted outside, checking for clearances.

"We need to get them out of there," Fet whispered.

"We need to figure out how we're going to take down

the building," Spider replied.

"I've got that covered. We just need to get rid of the guards."

Spider watched her for a moment before his eyes grew wide. "You're not actually going to blow it up, are you?"

"What choice do we have?"

"How are you going to do that?" he gasped, "you don't even have materials to make a bomb."

"We're not making a bomb, Spider, we're causing an explosion."

His eyes focused on her as she pulled out her device, her fingers flying over the screen as fast as his own typically worked. He knew he could outsmart her, he had done it before, but it was entrancing to watch her work without a screen and codes between them.

"There. I found it. Now I just have to get in." She frowned as she hit a block.

Spider brought his device to life, joining in on the fun.

"Allow me." His suddenly-much-deeper voice prompted Fet to look up at his newfound chivalry.

As they worked together, breaking through each wall, their keystrokes became more frantic, as if every time they made a move, someone specifically blocked them from continuing.

"Are you getting this?" Fet whispered loudly,

concerned over what entity they might be facing and how they so quickly knew her every move.

Spider didn't answer, intently typing away on his device, nearly matching Fet's every move.

"Who are we up against?" she whispered.

Fet's blonde hair fell in front of her face and she used the back of her wrist to swipe it away. Clearly the person holding Peep was not behind this blockade. Did that mean someone else knew what was happening and was trying to stop them?

"Still with me, Fet?" Spider taunted, a smug sneer creeping onto his face.

A few strokes later, she looked up, triumph written in her grin. "Nope," she said, "I'm already in."

Spider's head whipped up.

"How?" he stammered.

"I'll never tell." She arched her eyebrows, daring him to take her on. "Now, we need to move the guards."

She typed for a moment as Spider continued to stare, his eyes slowing to trace over her from head to toe, his fashion-opposite.

Fet's device started vibrating. The arrogance drained from her face as she lifted it.

"Spider, we have to move. Now!"

In his confusion, he stumbled, attempting to follow along behind her as he put his own device back into his pocket.

"What are you doing?" he yelled as he realized they were headed directly at the tall white building that loomed in front of them. Its modern, arched edges were anything but welcoming.

"We're on the clock, Spider. We have less than one minute to set off the explosion," she said as she tried to type while she ran. "There, the meltdown has started. All of the badges had already swiped out of the building when the power source went down, apparently it was all hands on deck, so there are only the guards left."

The first of the explosions filled the air, pieces of the back of the building floated to the ground. The noise pulsed around them, shocking their senses as they ran.

Fet nearly lost her footing as she realized they were about to make a mistake. Spider showed no signs of slowing.

"Wait, get down!" Fet yelled as they approached the terrifying scene. "They can't see you."

She intentionally tripped Spider, sending him crashing to the earth as she ran ahead.

"Fet, no!" he yelled, reaching to her from his place in the grass. "You can't die, no one will be able to save Peep!"

Ignoring his call, Fet ran as quickly as she could in her tall combat boots, pink skirt jostling around her as she rushed forward. She raced toward the building, feet pounding against the pavement as she hit the blacktop.

Spider couldn't hear the words she shouted to the guards as he stumbled to his feet and raced after her.

The second explosion rang out as the confused guards ran from the building, heeding whatever warning Fet had imparted on them. Debris rained down on her, like stars falling from the sky in a mass exodus of space. She rolled as she hit the ground, launching herself to her back to her feet and continuing on, only a slight limp as evidence of the danger she had been in.

Spider grabbed her arm as he reached her and dragged the girl away from the men who were turning for an explanation. Putting as much distance between them as possible, he only ducked when the third explosion sounded in the distance.

When he collapsed into the tall grass, his devices tumbled from his pocket.

"Thanks," Fet breathed when she stopped gasping. Her hand stretched the length of her leg to her ankle, checking for injuries.

"Have you lost your mind?" he yelled. "You could have died!"

"And if I hadn't, *they would have*!" she shrieked back, suddenly angry.

She reached for his device, picking it up off the ground to hand to him.

"I'll get it." Spider said quickly, reaching for it.

"Wait." Fet's brow knitted together. Something felt off.

"You used this. How could you use this? Your device went down when I killed the power."

Matching her face, he looked at her. "I.... I don't know."

"But..."

"We don't have time to figure it out, Fet. We have to get away from The Lab." Pieces of the building floated between them, catching in Fet's pigtail. Spider used his hand to brush away a piece of ash caught in his long eyelash.

"Over there!" a voice shouted—a guard looking for the young girl who had appeared out of nowhere as the explosion took place.

"We have to go," Spider whispered harshly.

"Not yet. We're not done here."

"But The Lab has been destroyed," he insisted, pulling at her arm.

"Not yet." Fet rose, allowing the guards to run beyond them before she doubled back. "I left one room standing. It's the backdoor into Irex."

"What?" Spider followed along behind her.

"It's how we take it back. The man who created it... He left a way into it that not even the government knows about. You need to wait here," she replied.

"Not a chance." Spider refused to back down.

The building was in shambles, walls standing at odd angles, pieces still falling off. Fet raced into the debris, careful to avoid the hot mental from the machinery. On the far side stood a confusing array of partial walls and hanging lights.

"There's a guard," Spider pointed out.

"Then take care of him," Fet hissed, pushing him toward the man as she disappeared around the wall.

The system had been partially damaged but enough remained that she could hack it. Fingers flying across the keyboard, she set to work establishing the break in the code needed to take back the Irex when the time came. Her head jerked up as a scream came from behind the wall, but she couldn't stop. Something very bad was happening, but she didn't know if Spider had caused it or experienced it.

The final stroke allowed her access. It was done.

Rounding the corner she found Spider leaning against the wall, waiting, face grim.

"What did you do?" her voice was low and terrifying as she realized where she stood in this little game.

"What did *you* do?" he challenged. Everything about him was so dark that he looked like a different person.

She couldn't trust him. She never should have to begin with. He was a hacker...he had destroyed her job once before. He had no remorse and no reason to help her.

His leather-bound hand dragged through his hair as he watched her, eyes narrow.

"Did you hurt that guard?" she demanded.

"No, I scared him off though." His gaze was icy. "What did you do, Muffet?"

"I enacted a program that lets me gain control over Irex," she responded.

"What program?"

"It's called the Way, and that's all you need to know."

He looked at her as if he loathed every bit of her. Sneering at the girl, he held her gaze, his shoulders rolling back as if he wanted to be anywhere but near her.

Suddenly, Spider's eyes softened just enough to be visible and he leaned toward her again, frightening her. Just as suddenly, his posture stiffened once more, reclaiming his icy distance.

"You need to tell me what's going on..." his voice was cut off as a small series of pops made Fet lunge forward.

"The last detonation is going to go off, move!" she charged at him, pulling him away before the last burst.

A sharp pulse moved through her hip as another mission came through.

"Return to the Hub." The words scrolled across her screen when she retrieved it. She realized she still didn't have an explanation for Spider's device suddenly working again. Nothing could be trusted.

"What could they possible need us *there* for?" Spider asked. No one answered as they continued to run.

THE MOON WASHED THE WORLD IN A white light as they approached the center of town. Sneaking passed the Legends building, hidden in plain sight, Fet realized she had never contacted T with information. She couldn't afford to now.

The Hub was still chaotic as the Coats were setting up their new home in the center of the town, having seen evidence of the explosion at their home base. Guards filled the area, keeping people back, weapons poised for use.

Faces in the growing crowd appeared. Fet caught BB's eye and shook her head to warn him off. Glancing quickly toward Spider, she hoped she had sufficiently warned the others. BB pulled back, drifting into the masses as the others slowly followed.

"We have to deal with the Irex, don't we?" Spider asked. A curt nod was the only response she gave him.

"Use Way to disable it from here," he said as she started forward, grabbing at her arm.

"Can't. Need the wires." Pushing past him, she forced her way into the crowd, refusing to tell him her plan. People jostled against her, knocking her off balance.

The air crackled, revealing a tense standoff between the people surrounding the building looking for answers and the watchmen guarding it. They held a barrier, attempting to block the people from getting to close. A man demanded answers, only to be pushed back.

A guard yelled, imploring everyone to stay away while the Coats worked. Tired of waiting for hours, the people jostled against one another, ready to take the men on. They had never experienced trouble with their technology like this before. Nothing had ever been shut down for so long. The disruption in the life they knew caused them to become caustic.

Fet filtered between people, making her way to where she could see a path into the building. Quietly, she slipped by, attempting not to be noticed with her loud outfit and eye-catching hair. Taking an elbow to the stomach, she pushed further, until she came to a less crowded area.

"Stop," a voice yelled. The weapon was raised at a child.

"Don't." she warned, stepping between the guard and the boy.

The boy flinched behind her. The guard lashed out,

catching Fet's arm, missing its mark. Fet fell to the ground, blood already pooling beneath her. She kicked, sending the guard crashing to the ground beside her. A second man ran to assist as a person in the crowd snatched up the child. The darkly clothed person hustled the boy away as Fet scrambled to leave the scene. Clutching her arm, she ran around the building directly into a Coat.

"I'll be needing that." Fet said as her good arm darted out in front of her. She touched the man's neck and he dropped, the pressure point knocking him out. Shrugging on the man's coat, she forced herself to walk slowly into the building. Making sure she was alone, she slipped inside.

The Hub was filled with Coats, all testing equipment and trying to right the situation. The low hum of technology filled the air as they used a generator to try to reestablish the connection. She took the stairs two at a time as she made her way to the remaining Irex system, hoping to make it behind closed doors before the blood started to show through the coat.

Powering the Irex through her own device, she sifted through everything that had happened.

"This makes no sense," she mumbled as numbers filtered across the screen. After a few moments she gasped. "It can't be. It's the Wall job."

"You're even better in person, Fet." Spider's voice

grated against her ears, her shoulders hunching in disgust as he entered the room behind her.

"I *knew* you had something to do with this. It was all too convenient."

"I saw what you did, Muffet. You protected those guards at The Lab and you took an attack for that child. Two men are dead out there. This chaos is getting people killed," he said, hands in his pockets.

"Who sent you, Spider?"

"The Piper."

Color drained from her face as the name hung between them.

"What does the Piper have to do with this?"

"The Barrier was his design. The government took it over and forced him out. He wants it back. This is his escape plan. The Wall job was just part of it. He designed it to see if the Legends could handle it."

"To see if *I* could handle it," she corrected.

"Yes," he nodded solemnly, giving her more information than she thought he should be, as her enemy. "He needs the leader of the Legends to finish this."

"Why are you telling me this?" she asked, still kneeling in front of the console.

"People are dying now. I won't be a part of that."

"Suddenly you're working with me? I don't buy it."

"I've known what was going on from the start, Muffet. I was the one working against you at the Lab.

I've been working to bring down the Piper from the inside."

"You honestly expect me to believe you're a triple agent?" her glare stopped him. "I get that spiders have eight legs, but not even *you* are capable of juggling that much. Careful, or I'll start ripping those legs off."

"You don't have to. I'll do it *for* you," he disregarded her warning. He took a dangerous step closer as he prepared to confess, hoping she would believe him. "I ruined the Wall job for you, but I gave you a way into the system. You're going to need that. Piper thought I was doing as he asked, but I created a backdoor into *your* system so I could see what you were doing and help you work against him. That's how I got in with the Legends to begin with. I knew your every move. I've watched you every day since that job. I know every keystroke you've made."

Fet stood, hands clenched at her sides, ready to attack if he got too close.

"I know you've never hurt anyone. *Piper has.* My family has been working against him from the start. We worked against the Legends too, until I watched you this past year. We stopped fighting you months ago. Didn't you realize when your life got suddenly easier?"

Her blood boiled at his words. He had no right to watch her.

How much time had he spent observing her every move?

How much did he know about her? How much did she want him to know about her?

He held her gaze, refusing to admit anything. She had no idea he knew so much more than she'd ever know. For an entire year he had memorized her every keystroke, every flourish, every movement. He knew every step she would take before she decided to take it. Her reactions were second nature to him.

Stepping forward, she swung at him. Catching her wrist, he pulled her close, leaning her backwards just far enough that if she moved, they would fall.

He held on to her, trying to control the situation and force her to listen to him.

"I'm not fighting you, Muffet," he growled, inches from her face.

Fet tried to decide if she could believe him. The way her body relaxed suggested she could, but her head screamed that she was crazy for giving in so quickly. She charted everything he had done in between breaths. Her mind whirred through everything he could have interfered with since the Wall job. Had he helped her? Every coincidence suggested he might have been with her all along.

"Then what are you doing?" She couldn't look him in the eye. He was too close.

"Helping you end this." Righting her, he refused to let

go of her waist, fingers lingering against her side. "Now finish disabling the Irex. Our next stop is the Wall."

"You mean it's a real place?" she asked, relinquishing the last brain cells that held out against him, hoping she hadn't misplaced her limited trust in him. She lowered herself to her knees in front of the wires she needed to manipulate and waited for the sound of a weapon against her skull as she turned her back to him to work, but nothing came.

"It's a very real place. And you're the only one who can finish it there."

"What does he want from me?" she asked as she carefully removed the wires from their rightful place.

"Your code. When the program was developed, a code was put in by the leader of the Legends. You have that code and he needs it to gain control back."

She didn't have the code. Peep had the code, passed down by the leaders of the group over the years.

"Back when he was working with the Legends, he trusted them with the final piece, a piece not even he knew, in order to protect the system. But now, with the way the government is...he just wants to get out, and bring the government down in his wake."

"The same government who is willing to kill innocent bystanders if they appear to threaten their reign at the command of the Coats?"

"Yes. Do you need help?" he asked, peering around her.

"I eat codes for breakfast, Spider, and I certainly think I can handle some cords and Way." She rolled her eyes, making him stifle a smile behind her back.

He watched as she carefully unplugged every wire and shut the system down.

"We're coming back for that, aren't we?"

"It's not like we're running away when this is all over," she huffed, brushing past him. "Now where is this ridiculous Wall?"

CHAPTER 5

"PEEP IS ON THE OTHER SIDE of the Wall, isn't she?" she stared up at the tall, metallic barrier.

"Yes."

The sleek silver glinted in the moonlight, a pale blue tone reflecting off of it menacingly.

"How do we get in?"

"You break the code," he answered. "There's a panel somewhere that we have to find. You need to plug in your code to open the door."

"Why exactly are you so eager to have me plug this code in? I thought you were working against him," she whispered as she judged the distance from the tall grass to the Wall.

"He has almost complete control now. We have to break in and take control back. And Fet..." he paused, catching her eye. "My brother is in there with Peep. I have a lot to lose, too."

"You risked your brother to work against the Piper?" she asked, suddenly softening to him.

"We need to end this."

"Peep is the head of the Legends," she admitted, shock registering on Spider's face. "I don't have the code."

"Then we hack it. Together," he collected himself. "Careful what you say when we walk out of here. He can hear."

Spider stalked out of the tall grass. Fet jumped up and raced behind him, boots pounding against the dirt. They separated ways, searching for the panel.

"Here," Spider called.

"Welcome, Muffet. Break the code and you can have her back," a taunting voice rang out. "Just plug your code in and she'll be free to go."

"Arach too." Spider shouted as he pulled off the panel.

"You really want your traitorous brother back, Spider? He lied to you. He worked for the enemy. He nearly got you caught. If I hadn't have saved you, you would have been tangled in his web of lies too. Unless..." the voice paused, as he realized he had been tricked. "...you're one of them, aren't you? Well. I didn't see that coming." He kept his voice even as he talked, refusing to show his feelings on the topic.

"The *Piper* didn't see that coming? What a fool! I thought Pipers knew all." Fet taunted as she plugged in her device and started typing along with Spider.

"Ridiculous girl. The world *follows* the Piper–" he started.

"–right to their destruction," Spider yelled, cutting him off.

"Nevertheless, you have to use your code if you want your people back. Don't think you can outsmart me; I have the Irex."

"Shut up if you want us to break your precious Wall." Fet yelled, glaring at the blinking camera hanging above them.

A panel slid away above them, allowing them to see the Piper's face, piercing green eyes overtaking the screen as he grinned at them.

"So feisty, Muffet. However do the Legends get anything accomplished with a leader like *you*?"

"We don't," her voice mingled with Spider's.

"They don't." he said at the same time, revealing that Fet wasn't their leader.

Piper's face fell as he realized his mistake.

"*You knew*," he accused.

"Not until just now. The Legends did a great job of keeping their leader quiet...even from me," Spider sneered as he typed, not bothering to look up at the screen.

"You'd better pray you can figure out the code then, or your people are dead," Piper threatened.

"Spider, get out!" a voice yelled in the background, forcing Spider away from his work.

"Pay attention!" Fet hissed as her fingers pounded against the keyboard.

Spider's head snapped back down. He moved closer to Fet so that their inside legs touched, making them a connected team. Whispering quietly, they tossed commands to each other. "Just like last year."

She nodded at his final idea, tied to the Wall job from the previous year. Code streamed out of them, attacking the system. The Irex backdoor allowed Fet to sneak into the system another way without being detected while Spider finished the assault that Piper could see.

"Who is your leader, Muffet?" Piper called, demanding answers. "If you fail, I'll kill them both."

"Not if we kill you first," Spider replied, bravado overcoming him.

"Tell me who it is!" he demanded.

"Send them out first," Spider retorted.

"I have the code!" Fet yelled satisfactorily. "Send them out!"

"System override in one minute," the system's digital voice penetrated the conversation, setting a timeline in motion they hadn't realized they initiated when they attempted to access the Wall's program.

"Send them out or you'll lose control of the system forever," Fet said smugly at the camera.

"Code first."

"People first," Fet insisted, brushing her hands against

her skirt in defiance. She crossed her arms over her chest and waited.

The screen went blank, but Fet stared it down.

A door to her left slid open revealing Peep and Arach being held by guards.

"Code, Muffet, then you can have your pathetic friends back."

"You're so willing to kill for what you want. Is it worth it?" she fired back, unwilling to move.

"*Fet,*" Peep warned, glaring.

"Gaining my freedom back? Yes. It's worth it. After what they did to me...they deserve it." Piper sneered as he lit back up on the screen. "They took everything from me."

"Says the man in a walled-in compound."

"My price for my silence," he shrugged, glancing at his prize. "No matter though. It will all be over soon and I can live anywhere I like. I'll control everything."

"You used to protect people," Fet challenged. "That's why I'm here, isn't it. Your little failsafe for keeping the system and people protected. What changed?"

"They did. They took everything from us. So what if there are a few deaths along the way to taking back our system from them? I'm going to set everyone free."

"By ruling over them?"

"I can keep them safe," he answered.

"By controlling them?"

"By controlling you *all*." He smiled as if he believed his words weren't merely a cry for power. "Now finish it."

"Fet, don't you dare!" Peep cried as she struggled against the guards. Arach locked eyes with Spider, trying to sense his plan.

"System override in ten seconds."

Alarms shrieked. Fet was surprised there weren't flashing lights to add to the drama of it all.

"Now or never, *Muffet*." Piper yelled as the guards raised their weapons to their captives.

Fet nodded to Spider and they turned back to the panel.

The code spun passed the screen, falling into place as the system exploded across the interface. Fet pressed the final keys.

Code sparkled as it fell down on the screen, regrouping at the bottom.

"No!" Peep shouted, falling to her knees.

Arach threw his elbow back, colliding with the guard. Peep forced her way free. She ran back toward the compound in an effort to undo the damage Fet and Spider had created.

"Arach!" Spider yelled, indicating he should turn and catch her. The boy raced after Peep, wrapping his arm around her, pulling her toward the exit. Spider held the door open, bracing himself between it and the wall as Fet charged forward, keeping the guards back. Arach dragged

Peep outside, leaping over Spider's legs as he forced the door open with his body. Fet darted over him just as the door forced Spider to drop. Fet pulled him along behind her, forcing him out of the way as the door slammed behind them, nearly crushing him.

"Run," Spider demanded, out of breath from holding the door open.

The four crashed through the tall grass, making their way away from the compound, anger rippling from Peep.

"How could you?" she shrieked when they slowed.

"Relax, Peep." Fet looked at her in disgust. "You have so little faith."

"She set up a back door," Spider said.

"And just who are you?" Peep demanded, whirling to face him.

"That's my brother." Arach announced.

"The one who works for Piper?"

"*Worked*." Spider corrected. "Double agent."

"Triple agent." Fet scoffed.

"Wait a minute. I know you. You're one of the *recruits*!" Peep scrutinized him.

"Can we skip that and get to the part about the back-door?" Arach cut in.

"Fet used the Irex to create a backdoor," Spider informed them.

"Irex?" Arach looked shocked.

"You went...?" Peep asked.

Fet nodded, giving them a quick rundown of their missions.

"Now we have to get back to the Hub and fix this."

"You're sure we can take him down?"

"Now that you're here, I'm positive. You've got the real code, after all." She grinned as Peep nodded.

"Well then, let's go run the Piper off a cliff."

They sprinted back to town, finding chaos still erupting between the people and the guards protecting the Hub.

"Stay here." Peep instructed, motioning them to remain in the shadows.

Spider and Arach mumbled quietly to each other. Fet only picked up a few words as they huddled together a few feet away discussing what had happened while they were separated. She glared when Spider kept glancing over to her, more frustrated than when his brother checked on her as well.

"What is she doing?" Spider eventually hissed.

"How should I know?" she bit back.

"Children." Arach cautioned, sensing an argument.

"Is that her?" Fet asked, looked beyond the brothers.

They turned, squinting to see who was approaching.

When Peep returned, she had a man at her side.

"He can get us in," she said, turning on her heels. Peep had contacts everywhere.

Without questioning her, the three followed behind

them, Spider terrifyingly close to Fet again. His hand brushed against her side as they walked up to the building. A door opened in front of them and Peep hesitated. Glancing at Fet, she made eye contact.

Fet nodded and Peep turned to the man holding the door. Spider and his brother were allowed access, officially being initiated into the Legends, all ceremony cast aside. The light of the early dawn was their only guide once inside.

"After you, Fet," the man whispered as she walked by him.

She froze in place before turning to him, studying his glasses.

"And you are?"

"You know me as Nim." His eyes sparkled as he revealed his identity. "These people know me as Jack."

A grin spread across her face.

"Our double agent." She nodded, letting her coolness slip away for a moment.

He pushed his glasses up on his nose, making him look even older than the decade he had on Fet.

"We've been watching each other a long time, haven't we?"

"We have." Fet glanced down the hall, making sure none of the other Coats were about to intrude. "Thanks for last month, by the way."

"I couldn't let my team walk into an ambush, now

could I?" He nodded that they should start down the corridor, whispering directions before peeling off down a side hall to avoid being caught with the group.

He shifted his gait as he walked away, making him nearly unrecognizable from the man who had just left them. The limp would easily throw any of the Coats who might identify him later. He was a man of many faces, as any good hacker would be.

Fet led the way up to the Irex, Peep attaching herself to Fet's side.

"Nim knows them." Peep hissed in her ear.

"Who?"

"Arach and Spider," she replied. "He's been watching them for a few months since the rest of their group was taken out."

"What happened?" Fet leaned in as quickly as Nim had just walked away.

"Nim's been covering for us here with the Coats. He only let them get so close to us before he'd block them. He saw them get close to their group too, but since we have no connection to them, he didn't interfere. Obviously he regrets that now since only a few of them weren't caught or killed in the raid."

Peep's fingers tightened around Fet's arm, digging into her skin.

"He started watching them and says they are clear. We can trust them."

The conversation stopped short as they reached the room containing the Irex. All four hackers paused to look around before slipping into the room.

Fet and Peep attached the machine's cords back in place as Spider and Arach stood back, watching their hands work quickly over the wires.

"What did you use?" she asked.

"The Way," Fet answered, stepping back.

"Seriously? Your big plan was to *unplug the cords and use the Way?*"

"Just stop talking and take back the system," Fet snipped, waving her hand at her boss.

Peep rolled her eyes and set to work. Leaning against the wall with Spider and Arach, she waited for Peep to need her help. She watched as her friend strained over the console, fighting to gain control, taking long enough to make Fet nervous.

"Ready," Peep said loudly, forcing Fet to push away from the wall and join her.

Together they fought the system, adding new codes and changing the existing ones to destroy Piper's control.

"Spider!" Fet demanded and he raced across the room.

His eyes flitted over the screen, bouncing across the numbers. Sliding in next to her, he started to work his magic on the system.

The room became stifling as they worked, their eyes

growing heavy from prolonged time looking at the screen. Arach watched quietly as his brother attempted to shatter the system.

"Almost there," Peep said.

"Don't even think about it." The voice made them jump.

Piper stood in the entranceway, his hand outside the door holding something. Men flanked him, waiting for their orders.

"I knew you couldn't resist doing something like this." He grinned. "So Peep, *you're* the real leader. I should have guessed. Your stupid act had me fooled. *Bravo.* But I'm still in control and you're going to step away."

His voice was gentle and easy; a terrifying combination when mixed with his harsh face.

"Not a chance," she growled.

A muffled cry from outside the door made Peep gasp.

Piper dragged BB in by the collar. His hands were bound in front of him, a gag in his mouth. He shook his head violently at Peep, warning her off.

"Oh, I don't think so," Spider snarled, launching himself at the man.

The guards attacked as Arach, Fet, and Peep joined the fight.

"Take out the machine!" Piper ordered.

Spider stopped the first guard with a well-placed fist to the throat. He recoiled, shaking his leather-covered hand. Arach managed to take out a second guard, a chair to the back of his head stopping him in his tracks.

Peep struggled to free BB as he pushed her back to the console. He worked, wrist still bound, alongside his girlfriend as the others fought to keep the men back.

A guard pulled on Fet's pigtail, jerking her head violently to the side.

"Fet!" Spider shouted, attacking the man who had her. Fet was thrown against the wall as Spider slammed into the man. Pushing back her long hair, no longer restrained on one side, she kicked out at the man nearest to her, stopping him from taking a piece out of Arach.

"Almost there. Fet!" Peep yelled.

"Go!" both brothers yelled at the same time.

Fet ran to Peep's side, moving BB out of the way. He was no match for them when they paired up, even unbound.

"Ready?" Fet asked.

"Now!" Peep commanded. The system destroyed all ties to Piper's control. They had freed the system and destroyed the Irex, ensuring no one could control the Barrier program again.

Rage washed over Piper, causing his entire body to shake.

"*You* did this!" he shouted at Fet.

Running toward her, he flew through the air, suddenly landing on the ground. Spider pulled his leg back under him, not even shuddering as the man tripped over him. He rushed to Fet's side.

"Go!" he said, grabbing her shoulder. "Run!"

"But..." she protested, wanting to stop Piper once and for all.

"Go. Now," he commanded. "Arach..."

Arach latched on to Peep and BB, spinning them to the door. Pushing them, he forced the couple to run toward it.

"Fet, go. I will take care of him, but he can't catch you. Now move."

"No!" she said, irritated. She did not need protecting.

"Get out, now!" he yelled as one of them men started to stir.

He looked around, preparing for the fight.

"Arach, get her out of here."

"On it." His brother reached for Fet. She beat him away.

"Fet," Spider grabbed her shoulders. "You need to go now. I can take care of this. I'll find you when it is safe, but he can't catch you. He will kill you, or use you to do his bidding, and I don't know which is worse. Just go. *Go!*"

Terror raced through her as he screamed at her, the wildness in his eyes prompting her to listen. She ran.

Arach followed behind her. She couldn't remember running down the stairs, but she found herself on the ground floor, running through the door.

BB was free from his binds by the time she reached them. He held Peep close as they waited for Arach and Fet to catch up. Peep shot them a look.

The watchmen swarmed the building, the Coats demanding they protect the technology and end the intruders.

"He stayed behind. We have to go." Arach supplied before she could ask. The chaos in the building they had run from increased, terrifying Fet to her core. Who would survive?

BB LED THE WAY AS THEY RAN TO THE Legends building, ducking within its walls. Everyone was relieved to see Peep back. She explained what had happened, introducing Arach as a new member of the group. Everyone listened intently as they manned their stations, looking for fallout from Piper.

Fet wander to the edge of the building. She slipped passed the recruits' room into an isolated area near the door. Oppressive silence followed in her footsteps, making her thoughts that much louder as they ricocheted around in her brain.

It was her fault. He never should have stayed behind for her. If he died, that would be on her hands.

She paced, each step making her combat boots feel heavier. Her hand found it's way to her pigtail, coiling it around her fingers as she tried to steady herself, convincing her overactive mind that it would all work out.

"He'll be all right." Arach's soft voice sounded eerily like Spider's as he slipped into the stuffy room.

"You're sure?" she asked, letting down her tough façade.

"He hasn't failed me yet. I know he doesn't look as buff as me," he paused to grin, "but trust me, he's been trained well. Besides, if he could defeat *you*, don't you think he could defeat *Piper*?"

"*Hey!*" she gasped as he threw the Wall job in her face. What was with these brothers?

"He'll be fine. And even if he's not, it's not your fault. He knew what he was getting into when he started obsessing over you."

"He obsessed over me?" she shot him a smug look.

"Long pigtails, pink skirts, shoes as tall as his, and a top hacker to boot? Yeah. He was obsessed." Arach grinned. "Anyway, let me know when he gets back."

He sauntered away, hands in his pocket, apparently unconcerned that his brother had just taken on a villain and his goons alone. Watching him, she realized how much they looked alike, even though Arach was more muscular and his hair was short cropped. She was amazed at what a good team they had been.

Silence overtook the room again, the life leaving with Arach. Her fingers ached to find a screen with code so she could stop thinking and focus on something else. Only her breathing filled the silence.

"You don't have to worry about him. The authorities have him."

Everything stopped.

She nodded, not trusting herself to face him.

"You scared me back there," she finally announced.

"I know." Spider took a step closer.

Giving in, she pushed away from the table she was perched on and turned to him.

"Your arm..." she began as she caught sight of him.

"I'm fine," he stopped her, shifting to take the focus off the blood that mirrored her own. Matching scars from their first mission as a team would be a lasting reminder.

"How did...?"

"I stopped him and handed him over. That's all you need to know."

"I need to know what you said to that guard at the Lab..." She crossed her arms, wincing as she felt the pain from her injury she had yet to tend to.

"You should get that looked at," Spider grinned, taunting her.

"You should too, *pest*."

"You want to look at it for me?" he challenged.

"Ha. *You wish*, Spider," she said sarcastically, as he stepped toward her, closing the distance.

"Yeah, I do." His voice was hard, as if the words physically hurt to say them. Ice dripped like sharp knives falling from his lips as he admitted he didn't despise her. The dark-haired boy waited for her ridicule. Giving in before she could end her silence, he raised his good hand and tangled it in her free falling hair.

"*I* heard you're obsessed with me," she mocked him, his lips turning down as his eyes narrowed.

"I'll squash him like a bug." Spider sneered, knowing it was his brother who had sold him out. She smiled as he leaned closer.

"You're a real jerk, you know that?" Fet said, refusing to lean any closer.

"You have no idea," he replied, wrapping his injured arm around her. "You can find out though. But no more running away, okay? And *I know*, I *told* you to..."

He rolled his eyes, knowing she would call him out for sending her away. She cut him off.

"*Hmm...* Didn't like that part?" she taunted quietly, smirking. He shook his head as he moved so close his lips were nearly brushing hers. "Don't worry, I'm pretty much caught in whatever web you've spun, Spider."

"Good, because we're nowhere near done with this thing yet. Piper may be arrested, but the fallout from this has only just begun."

ACKNOWLEDGMENTS

I sincerely hope you all enjoyed meeting Fet and Spider. I had a ball writing these two. Their fashion sense is probably my favorite thing about them, but let's be real, I love a good hacker story, too!

The good news is that because the fans pushed really hard, there's more to Spider and Fet's story! You can check out the sequel, And They'll Come Home, which is from Peep and Arach's side of things now, and then you can get more in the Legends Chronicles series, which is coming out soon!

If you're loving not he world of the Legends, drop me a line and let me know. Just about everyone in this series is a nursery rhyme character, and I'd love to hear about who you want to see more from!

In case you didn't know, Along Came A Spider was a bit of a surprise. No one knew I was dropping this short story until it released. I can't even tell you how fun keeping this a secret has been! Let me know if you'd like to see more of this in the future!

Special thanks to Alexis for being the first to read Muffet and Spider's story and loving it. The fan art before the book was even known to anyone was awesome!

Thank you to Awnna Marie Evans, my lovely editor, for ensuring none of my characters were turned into a Cyclops because I brilliantly missed a letter at the end of a word. You rock!

To the lovely Sissy Lu for all your help with my little secret. You're amazing, as always!

Special shout out to my Elite Street Team. Thank you for putting up with me taunting you over this little secret for an entire month before I started dropping hints to the public about my announcement. I'm not going to lie, it was really fun!

To you, oh wonderful reader, thank you for jumping into this journey with me. I can't wait to see where it takes us! Until then, I hope you come hang out with me on social media. I have a gift for you over on my newsletter if you enjoy excerpts from my other books and full books, as well as other freebie gifts. Come join me at excerpt.kmrobinsonbooks.com I can't wait to hang out with you!

Keep reading for a first look at more Legends Chronicles, as well as find out how to get bonus scenes, play an interactive game for Along Came a Spider and more!

Stay inspired,

-K.M. Robinson

AND THEY'LL COME HOME: THE FIRST PREQUEL NOVELETTE TO THE LEGENDS CHRONICLES

Little Hacker Peep
was taken from her sheep
and they don't know where to find her.
They won't leave it alone,
they'll bring her home
and they'll drag the Piper behind them.

WHEN PEEP, the leader of hacker group, the Legends, is abducted and held for ransom, she must try to help her best friend, Muffet, to find where she is being held at the Wall and save her people without giving away her true role in the group.

· · ·

WHEN ARACH IS SEPARATED from his brother, Spider, he must continue to play the Piper's game, convincing him that what remains of his family is working for the villain they are trying to destroy, all while convincing his former rival, Peep, to trust them as he tries to untangles their web of lies.

Get the sequel at
atchinfo.kmrobinsonbooks.com

THINK you have what it takes to join Fet and Peep in the Legends? Fet will put you to the test in this choose-your-own-adventure game through Facebook messenger to see if you have the skills to talk your way into the group.

Play now at jointhelegends.kmrobinsonbooks.com
and see if you can *hack* it.

BONUS FACEBOOK FILTERS

Want to get your hands on some incredible Facebook filters for Along Came A Spider? Now you have the ability to get filters for the story, characters, etc right inside your phone.

You can use these on your photos, profile pictures, videos, and live broadcasts. All you have to do is like my author page and they will automatically show up in your filters!

I've even taken these clips and put them on Instagram Stories by saving them to my phone and uploading them to Instagram.

Visit www.facebook.com/kmrobinsonbooks to grab these filters for your photos, videos, and broadcasts!

Bonus points for tagging me @kmrobinsonbooks so I can see how you're supporting The Legends Chronicles.

ABOUT THE AUTHOR

K.M. Robinson is a storyteller who creates new worlds both in her writing and in her fine arts conceptual photography. She is a marketing, branding and social media strategy educator who is recognized at first sight by her very long hair. She is a creative who focuses on photography, videography, couture dress making, and writing to express the stories she needs to tell. She almost always has a camera within reach.

CONNECT ON SOCIAL MEDIA

facebook.com/kmrobinsonbooks

instagram.com/kmrobinsonbooks

twitter.com/kmrobinsonbooks

Get free excerpts and full novels from K.M. Robinson at excerpt.kmrobinsonbooks.com

ALSO BY K.M. ROBINSON

The Golden Trilogy

Book One: Golden

Forged: A Golden Novella

Book Two: Locked

Book Three: Edge

The Complete Series Boxset/Omnibus with Tempered: an
exclusive bonus novella

The Jaded Duology

Book One: Jaded

Book Two: Risen

The Complete Series Boxset/Omnibus with exclusive epilogue

The Siren Wars Saga

Book One: The Siren Wars

Book Two: Darker Depths

Book Three: Beyond The Shores

Origins of the Siren Wars: Prequel Novella

Book Four: Forbidden Waters (coming soon)

The Legends Chronicles

Along Came A Spider: A Prequel Novelette

And They'll Come Home: A Prequel Novelette

The Archives of Jack Frost Series

The Revolution of Jack Frost

The Redemption of Jack Frost (coming soon)

Stealing Steam Series

Book One: Lions and Lamps

Book Two: Pistons and Prisoners

Book Three: Railcars and Rulers

Top Hats and Telegraphs: A Prequel Novella

The Complete Series Boxset/Omnibus with Vambraces and Victories: an exclusive bonus novella

Virtually Sleeping Beauty: A Novella Retelling

The Goose Girl and The Artificial: A Novella Retelling

The Sinking: A Little Mermaid Novella Retelling

Cindrill: A Cinderella Assassin Novella Retelling

Sugarcoated: A Hansel and Gretel's Witch Novella Retelling

Blood Is Silent: A Red Riding Hood Circus Retelling

JADED: BOOK ONE OF THE JADED DUOLOGY

If the only way to stay alive was to convince your new husband not to murder you and make it look like an accident, could you do it?

At eighteen, Jade shouldn't have to be forced to marry the son of her father's enemy as part of a revenge plot for a failed rebellion. When she's thrown into the life of being the wife of the Commander's son and heir, her only hope for survival is convincing Roan Diamond to actually fall in love with her so that he doesn't kill her on his father's wishes.

While a dutiful son, Roan shouldn't have to trick his new wife into believing his family accepts her, but as the only one in a position to make the country believe Jade is part of their family, he will do what he has to before his family murders his young bride and makes it look like an accident to get back at Jade's father.

With half the country trying to protect Jade and the other half oblivious to the atrocities committed at the Commander's hand, it's a race to see who will win at a deadly game of cat and mouse.

One chooses life. One chooses death. In the midst of chaos, only one will succeed.

Now available!
Learn more about The Jaded Duology at
jadedinfo.kmrobinsonbooks.com

**GOLDEN: BOOK ONE OF THE GOLDEN
TRILOGY**

**Goldilocks wasn't naive. She was sent on a mission and
Dov Baer is her new target.**

When Auluria tricks the Baers into letting her into their
home, they have no idea she's actually been sent by the
enemy to destroy them. Intent on gathering information
for her cousin to hand over to the Society seeking to
destroy all of the rebel factions—including her own—
she's willing to sacrifice Dov Baer to save her people...
until she realizes her cousin lied to her.

Now that she's seen who Dov truly is, she has to decide
between staying loyal to her only remaining family or
protecting the man she's falling for. If her allegiances are

discovered, either side could destroy her—assuming the Society doesn't get her first

Available now!

Learn more about The Golden Trilogy at goldeninfo.kmrobinsonbooks.com

**THE SIREN WARS: BOOK ONE OF THE
SIREN WARS SAGA**

War has hovered around the kingdom of Scylla for generations ever since the original sirens left the mer collection generations ago after nearly drowning the human prince. Over the years, select mermaids from the royal bloodline have been trained as spies to work for the reigning kings and queens, keeping the collection safe from sirens and humans.

Celena and her partner, Merrick, work covertly for the royals—not even her twin brother knows. When they discover the sirens have broken through the barriers the mer set up to keep the sirens out, Celena and her friends must race to the old kingdom of Metten to stop them from starting a war within their borders.

When she's dragged to the surface, Celena realizes that the war above the waters is as deadly as the one below the waves—and sacrificing herself may be the only way to protect her family.

The Siren Wars have only just begun.

Available now!

Learn more about The Siren Wars Saga at sirenwarsinfo.
kmrobinsonbooks.com

LIONS AND LAMPS: BOOK ONE OF THE STEALING STEAM SERIES

All wishes require sacrifice...*are you willing to pay the price?*

Cyra spent the last seven years being trained to steal an airship in a brutal competition that leaves the victor with millions. Last year, she won.

Aladdin spent the past year fighting to get enough money to take his mother away from Horallen after his father was murdered. Now, his evil uncle Kacper wants to force him into the competition and straight to his death inside the Collection Cave.

When Aladdin discovers a genie said to have been banished a century ago, the competition becomes even deadlier, and he knows he can't trust the girl who snuck into the competition this year...but Cyra might not survive his ruthlessness either in a game where only the lion's heart can win.

All wishes require sacrifice, and someone is going to pay the price for the Stourbridge.

Available now!

Learn more about The Stealing Steam Series at

lionsandlampsinfo.kmrobinsonbooks.com

ALONG CAME A SPIDER: THE FIRST PREQUEL NOVELETTE TO THE LEGENDS CHRONICLES

Little Hacker Muffet

sat on her tuffet

destroying her cords and Way.

Along came a hacker named Spider,

who sat down beside her

and frightened his opponent away.

When Fet, one of the most skilled hackers in the Legends, discovers her best friend and leader of her group has been abducted and held for ransom, she must escape unnoticed and find Peep before it's too late.

When Spider, a new recruit training to join her hacker

ring, slips out with her and claims to have a plan to save her friend, Fet is forced to bring him along. As she discovers he's not who he claims to be, she faces grave danger and learns just how deadly a spider bite can be.

Now available!
Learn more about The Legends Chronicles at
acasinfo.kmrobinsonbooks.com

VIRTUALLY SLEEPING BEAUTY

T*o wake her up, he has to enter the game and help her beat it...*

SURELY THE CLASS president wouldn't illegally over-juice to stay in the virtual reality game citizens are allowed to play for four hours a day, but when Royce's aunt calls in a panic because her goddaughter hasn't left the game yet, his only option is to go inside the game and drag the girl out.

THE GOLDEN KNIGHT quickly discovers the princess' absence in the real world isn't of her own doing—*she's trapped inside the game by unknown forces*—and if she can't escape soon, she could die for real outside of the game. He's even more shocked to discover that Rora outranks him inside of the game, which means she'll have to fight to *protect herself* from the evils locking her inside a dangerous world.

CAN Rora and Royce work together to outsmart a vicious queen and evil magician, and defeat digital dragons, or will Rora slowly fade away until there's nothing left but an empty shell and the game ranking she will leave behind?

Now available!

Learn more about Virtually Sleeping Beauty at
vsbinfo.kmrobinsonbooks.com

THE REVOLUTION OF JACK FROST

No one inside the snow globe knows that Morozoko Industries is controlling their weather, testing them to form a stronger race that can survive the fall out from the bombs being dropped in the outside world—all they know is that they must survive the harsh Winter that lasts a month and use the few days of Spring, Summer, and Fall to gather enough supplies to survive.

When the seasons start shifting, Genesis and Jack know something is going on. As their team begins to find technology that they don't have access to inside their snow globe of a world, it begins to look more and more like one of their own is working against them.

. . .

GENESIS SOON DISCOVERS MOROZOKO INDUSTRIES, but when a foreign enemy tries to destroy their weather program to make sure their destructive life-altering bombs succeed in destroying the outside world, only one person can shut down the machine that is spinning out of control and save the lives of everyone inside the bunker —Jack.

Now available!
Learn more about The Revolution of Jack Frost at
jackfrostinfo.kmrobinsonbooks.com

THE GOOSE GIRL AND THE ARTIFICIAL

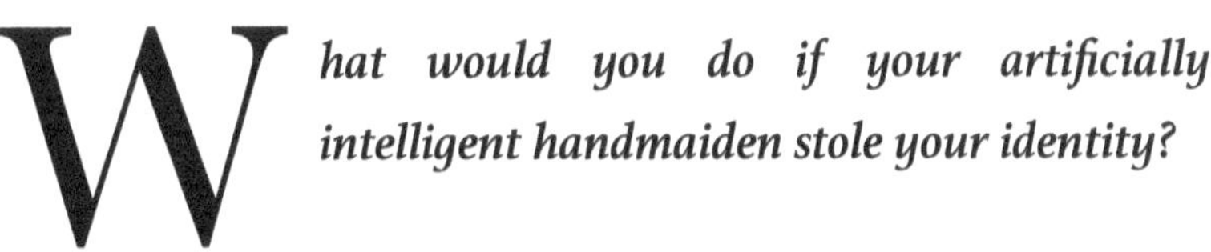

hat would you do if your artificially intelligent handmaiden stole your identity?

THREATENED BY HER ARTIFICIAL, Arta, Princess Goselyn is forced to switch places and pretend she isn't human when she reaches Prince Corinth to negotiate a treaty they both need to be able to take their respective crowns one day. If she doesn't comply, her Artificial, controlled by her evil cousin, will not only kill Goselyn's mother, but Prince Corinth and his father as well.

CAN the quiet princess outsmart a machine created to be

more intelligent than she is, all while surviving the other Artificials and robots working against her in the foreign palace, or will Corinth and his father find out and destroy her chance to save them all?

Learn more about The Goose Girl and The Artificial at goosegirlinfo.kmrobinsonbooks.com

THE SINKING

The sea witch wants to silence her, but not for the reason you think.

W hen a quirky older woman pawns a fancy seashell necklace at her mother's antique shop on the pier, Cara doesn't think much about the story the woman spins about the wearer turning into a mermaid.

On her way home, she accidentally drops the necklace into the ocean and is swept out to sea where she meets— a merman who volunteers to take her to his mother, the sea queen, to help her get her legs back.

.   .   .

CARA SOON LEARNS that it's Quay's eighteen birthday—a day that has been a curse for his family—and is meant to be one for her too. Now she must fight to survive the sea with Quay at her side.

Fans of The Little Mermaid will love this twisted take on the beloved story.

Now available!
Learn more about The Sinking at
thesinkinginfo.kmrobinsonbooks.com

CINDRILL

Cinderella is an assassin out to murder the prince...*but he's hunting her too.*

THE NANOBOTS CINDRILL'S master gives her to use as a mask allow her to slip into the ball wearing a face that isn't hers, but when the assassination attempt goes sideways, Prince Davin doesn't understand why her face changes when he injures her, slicing her foot open around a unique pair of shoes as she runs away.

WHEN CINDRILL RUNS into the prince the next day without her nanobot mask on, he doesn't recognize her, but immediately decides her skills will be useful on his hunt for the would-be-assassin woman who nearly killed his father and his fiancée the night before.

BOTH ARE TASKED with the job of murdering the other, but things don't quite go as they had planned when Cindrill's master and Davian's fiancée interfere as the two try to decide whether or not to kill the other.

IT'S hard to recognize a woman when she uses technology to change her appearance, but Cindrill is going to use that to her full advantage as she destroys the prince. ***Will either survive?***

Now available!

Learn more about Cindrill at
cindrillinfo.kmrobinsonbooks.com

SUGARCOATED

Hansel and Gretel's witch was actually on their side...

Annika's job is to create a cake to match the candy-colored rooftops, nightly firework shows, and daily parades ending in unexpected executions for the mad king's ball, but her true mission is to sneak a thirteen-year-old assassin into the palace using her gift of illusions.

Hansel's job is to protect his little sister, Gretel, once she assassinates King Levin and ends the destruction in Candestrachen, using his power over light to rescue the young girl from the chaos her influence over life and death will create.

.   .   .

WHEN THE ENTIRE forest reconstructs itself under Gretel's command while trying to save herself from a king's guard, Hansel and Annika must put their feelings aside and ensure their plan holds true—even if it means one of them has to sacrifice themselves to protect the mission.

Her illusions were meant to save her....but not everyone will survive the assassination attempt.

Learn more about Sugarcoated at
sugarcoatedinfo.kmrobinsonbooks.com

BLOOD IS SILENT

R*ed Riding Hood is a circus aerialist and the wolf is ready to cage her.*

SIENNA HAS GROWN up working for the circus, dangling off her signature red silks every night. Her grandmother has been known to wander off to train new acts for their boss, but when Sienna tries to find her to bring her back to the show, she doesn't expect the dashing and dangerous Elijah to join her.

WHEN they finally find Grandma Ida has been transformed deep in the heart of the woods, Sienna will stop at nothing to save her—but the wolf has her right where he wants her, and she won't be able to escape his claws.

She was told not to go into the woods alone.

Now available!

Learn more about Blood Is Silent at bloodissilentinfo.kmrobinsonbooks.com